DumP TrucK DISCO

Written by **Skye Silver**

Illustrated by **Christiane Engel**

Sung by **Audra Mariel**

Barefoot Books

step inside a story

Everything is quiet. Everyone's asleep.
But giant wheels are rolling softly up the street.

Dump Truck Daisy has come out with her crew. She's got a secret project. What's she going to do?

Lights blink on.
Engines go **VROOM!**
It's the dump truck disco...
ZOOM, ZOOM, ZOOM!

Garbage Truck Gertie clears away the trash
With a *shove* and a *PUSH*
and a *heave* and a *CRASH*
— *shhh!*

Dump Truck Daisy hauls in the dirt
And dumps it on the ground, then signals the alert.

Lights blink on.
Engines go **VROOM!**
It's the dump truck disco...

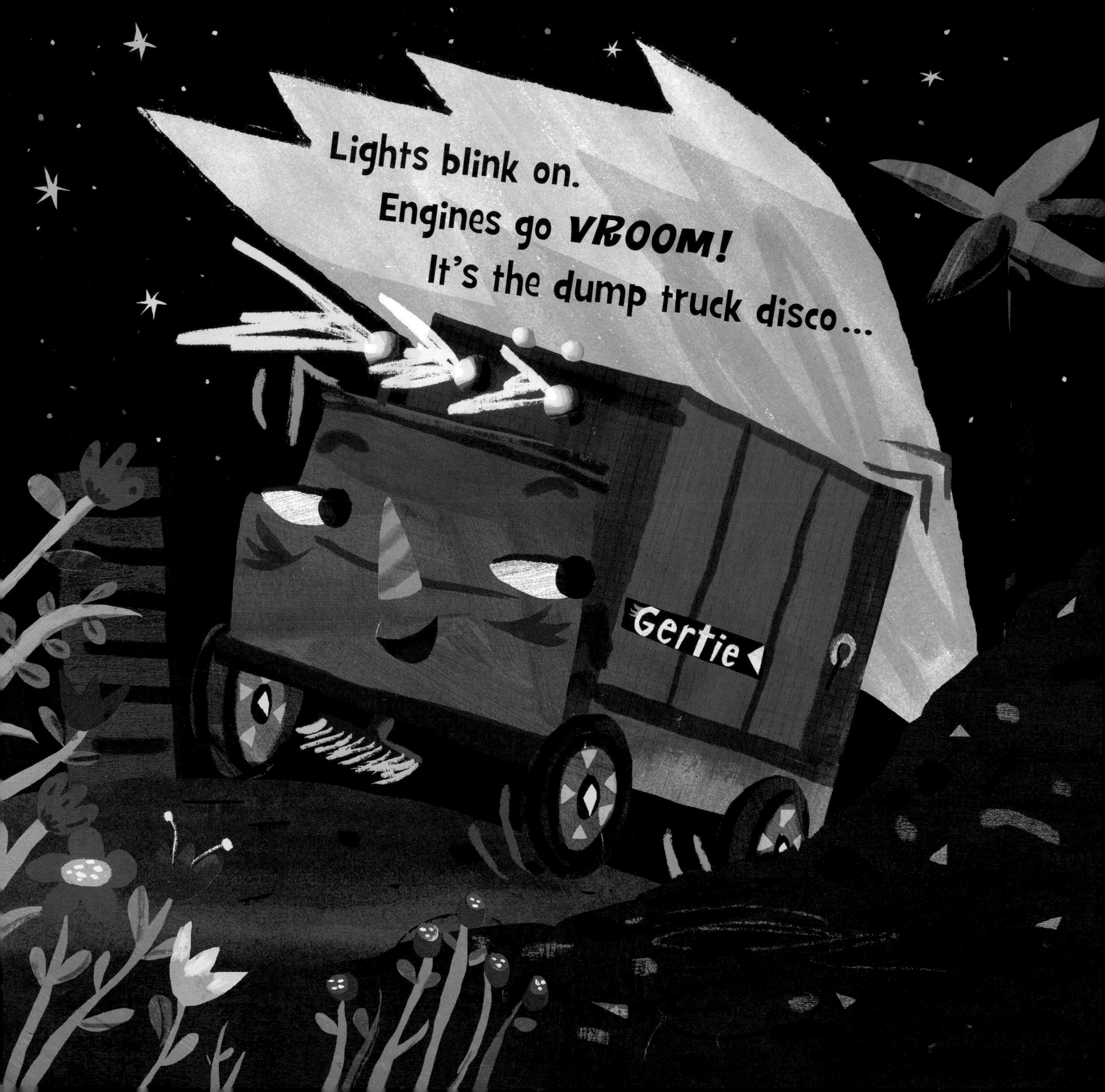

Bulldozer Beatriz levels out the ground. She *boogies* and she *woogies* but tries not to make a sound.

Excavator Esteban digs a big hole.
Scoop scoop, beep beep — now they're on a roll!

Lights blink on.
Engines go ***VROOM!***
It's the dump truck disco...

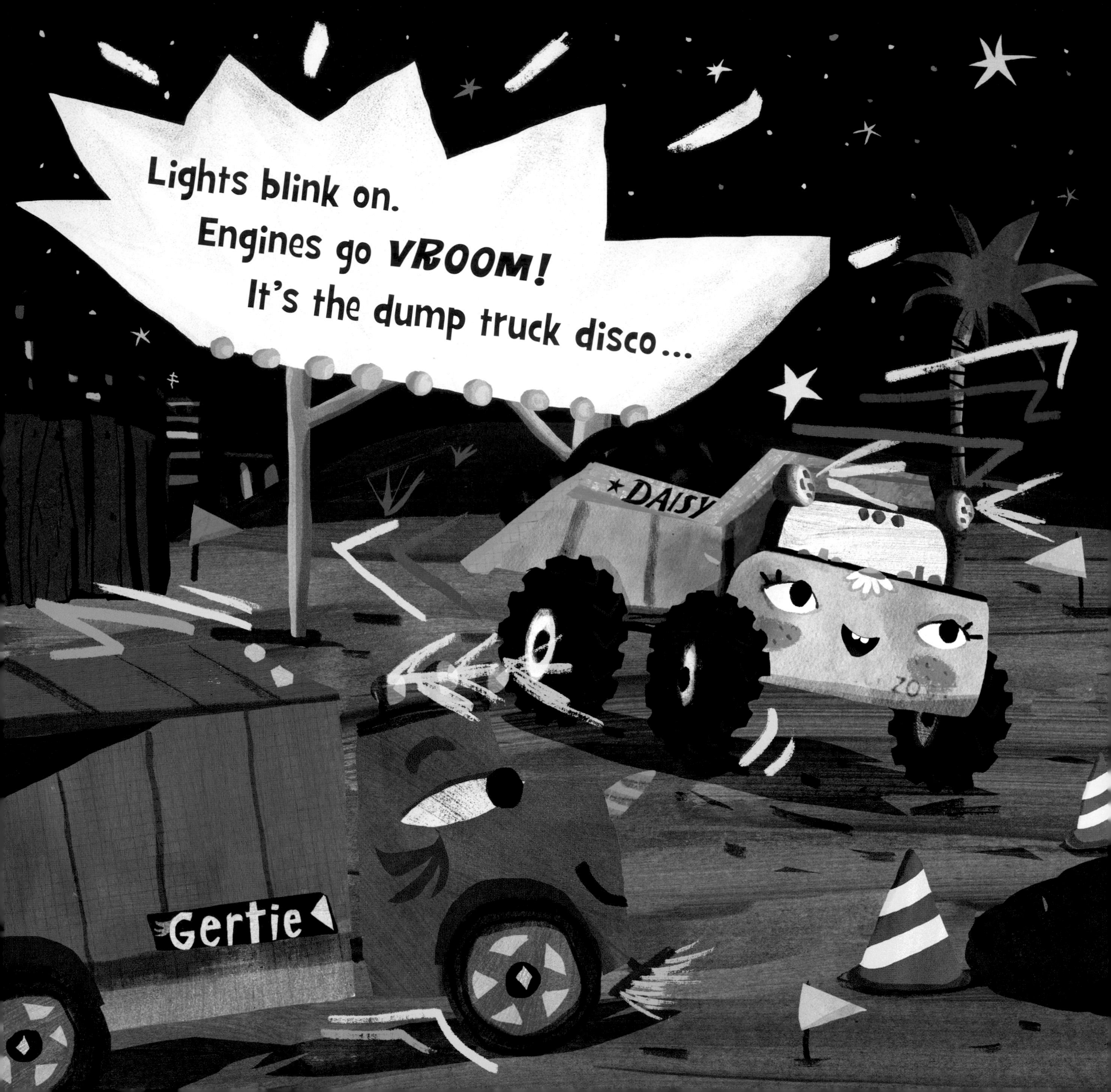

Mixer Max pumps a concrete base.
Tractor Tiana drags poles into place.

Kazuo Crane lifts equipment up high
And lowers it back down beneath the starry sky.

Lights blink on.
Engines go **VROOM!**
It's the dump truck disco...

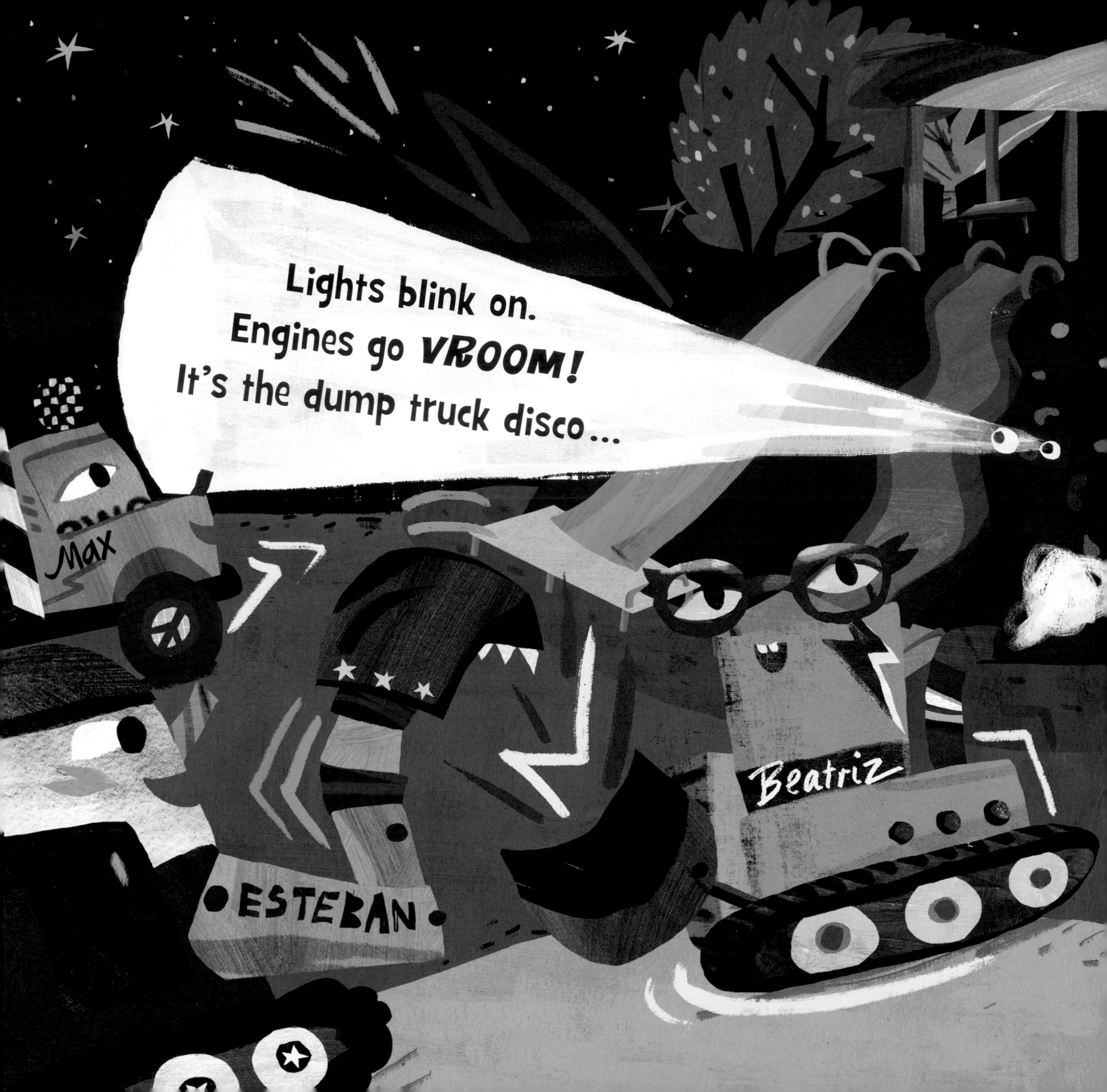

The moon has set. It's almost morning.
Dump Truck Daisy whistles out a warning.
It's time to clean up. It's time to go away.
It's time for the children to come along and play.

Lights blink off. Wheels stop spinning.
The crew heads home. A new day's beginning.

We all wake up and find a big surprise:
A brand new playground, right before our eyes!

We **SLiDE** and **SWING**. We **JUMP** and **SPiN**.
Let the all-day playground party begin!

Faces light up. We all go **VROOM!**
It's an all-day playground party...

We head home at last as the sun goes down.
Dump Truck Daisy is back in town.

Her crew is searching for another secret site...
What do you think they're going to build tonight?

Construction Vehicles

Can you come up with a different dance move for each construction vehicle?

robotic arm

hopper

Gertie

Garbage Trucks

Garbage trucks, also called trash or rubbish trucks, collect waste and carry it to landfill sites. Automated garbage trucks have a **robotic arm** that picks up bins and dumps their contents into the **hopper**, where a compactor crushes the garbage.

Dump Trucks

Dump trucks, also called tippers or dumper trucks, carry construction materials like sand, dirt or gravel on a flat **bed**. When the dump truck reaches the construction site, a rod pushes up the back of the bed, tipping it over and dumping the materials out.

bed

DAISY

ESTEBAN

arm

bucket

Excavators

An excavator, or a digger, has a big **arm** with a **bucket** on the end of it. The arm extends out to dig holes with the bucket. Excavators can also mine rocks, dredge up sand from rivers or even remove snow.

barrel

Mixers

Concrete mixers combine cement and water with sand or gravel to form the hard concrete used in many construction projects. Concrete mixers have a **barrel** that spins around to keep its contents blended together.

Max

Tractors

A tractor is designed to pull heavy things behind it. On a farm, it might drag a mower, while on a construction site it might haul a **trailer**. Tractor engines have to provide enough power to drive the tractor and to tow machinery.

trailer

TIANA

Bulldozers

Bulldozers use the **blade** mounted on the front to level the ground as they move. The band of plates around the wheels, called continuous track or **caterpillar track**, helps bulldozers drive over bumpy ground.

Beatriz

caterpillar track

blade

boom

Cranes

KAZUO

Cranes have an arm called a **boom** that can lift heavy things, lower them down or move them side to side. Cranes can be small enough to move boxes inside a room, or large enough to lift a sunken ship out of the ocean.

What makes a playground fun for everyone?

No two people are exactly alike. Great playgrounds are designed to be fun for everyone who visits!

The equipment is easy for everyone to get on and off.

A playhouse is perfect for make-believe.

Music stimulates the senses!

Everyone needs a quiet place sometimes.

Swinging and spinning can be good for the body and the brain.

Play zones marked by different floor types make it easier to find your way around.

Special thanks to **Magical Bridge Foundation** for providing expert input and for inspiring us with their playgrounds, which welcome visitors of all ages and all abilities. Thanks also to construction expert Heather Hayes Cavitt for reviewing the scientific accuracy of the book.

Barefoot Books
2067 Massachusetts Ave
Cambridge, MA 02140

Barefoot Books
29/30 Fitzroy Square
London, W1T 6LQ

Text copyright © 2018 by Skye Silver
Illustrations copyright © 2018 by Christiane Engel
The moral rights of Skye Silver and Christiane Engel have been asserted

Lead vocals by Audra Mariel
Musical composition © 2018 by Skye Silver and Michael Flannery
Musical arrangement © 2018 by Michael Flannery
Produced, mixed and mastered at Jumping Giant, New York City, USA
Animation by Sarita McNeil, Halifax, NS, Canada

First published in Great Britain by Barefoot Books, Ltd and in the United States
of America by Barefoot Books, Inc in 2018. All rights reserved

Graphic design by Sarah Soldano and Elizabeth Kaleko, Barefoot Books
Edited and art directed by Kate DePalma, Barefoot Books
Construction vehicle endnote text by Nivair H. Gabriel, Barefoot Books
Reproduction by Bright Arts, Hong Kong. Printed in China on 100% acid-free paper
This book was typeset in Century Gothic, Floraless, Grilled Cheese BTN and Hiroko
The illustrations were prepared in acrylics, water-based paints and digital collage

Hardback with enhanced CD ISBN 978-1-78285-407-4
Paperback with enhanced CD ISBN 978-1-78285-408-1
E-book ISBN 978-1-78285-612-2

British Cataloguing-in-Publication Data: a catalogue record
for this book is available from the British Library
Library of Congress Cataloging-in-Publication Data is available upon request

1 3 5 7 9 8 6 4 2